PRESENTING

LENNY AND LOLA

· MARC BROWN ·

A Unicorn Book　·　E. P. Dutton　New York

LIBRARY OF CONGRESS CATALOGING IN PUBLICATION DATA

Brown, Marc Tolon.   Lenny and Lola.
SUMMARY: The world's most famous trapeze duo stuns
their audience with a never-before-seen act.
[1. Circus stories]   I. Title.
PZ7.B81618Le [E]   77-16426   ISBN 0-525-33465-3

Published in the United States by E. P. Dutton, a Division
of Sequoia-Elsevier Publishing Company, Inc., New York

Published simultaneously in Canada by Clarke,
Irwin & Company Limited, Toronto and Vancouver

Editor: Emilie McLeod   Designer: Riki Levinson
Printed in the U.S.A.   First Edition
10 9 8 7 6 5 4 3 2 1

For my partner Stephanie,
with love and appreciation

Lenny and Lola were the most famous trapeze team in the world. People called them electrifying, stupendous, fantastic! They moved like the works of a beautiful clock.

Until the night Lola decided to put her solo into the act.

"Don't you ever do that again!" yelled Lenny.

"If that's the thanks I get for trying to improve the act, I'm leaving." And Lola walked out. Lenny stood alone in front of the astonished crowd.

"You can be replaced!" he shouted.

"Then you just find yourself a new partner."

Lenny began the search for a new partner.
He placed a full page ad in the newspaper.
It showed a large picture of him next to an
empty space and a question mark. It read:

THIS COULD BE YOU!
THE FANTASTIC LENNY
IS AUDITIONING NEW PARTNERS.

Daisy was the first to apply. She was agile but too heavy and had a bad habit of snapping her chewing gum.

Maurice caught on too quickly. He was very good. Too good. After only one week he got an act of his own and a fat contract with the Italian circus.

Lenny tried his nephew Arnold. He was very clumsy.

"This is not a comedy act," explained Lenny.

And so Lenny's act became a solo. It was good. With Lola, it had been terrific.

Tonight he was going to do what he had never done since Lola left. He was going to do his triples. He could do them alone.

His thoughts were interrupted by the ringmaster. "Five minutes, Lenny."

He walked alone to the rope ladder.
His silk cape rippled as he walked.

The clowns led the elephants from
the ring.

The tent was packed and quiet.

"And now, ladies and gentlemen, I present the fabulous, flying Lenny!" announced the ringmaster.

Lenny climbed high into the tent.

The audience cheered as he stood proudly on the platform.

He caught the swinging trapeze. Holding the bar firmly, he left the platform and swung.

His hands left the bar. The crowd gasped. One somersault.

Again his hands hit the bar. His timing was flawless. The trapeze had become a part of him.

A drum roll. Silence spread through the tent.

He was ready for the triples. He grasped the trapeze to swing out over the crowd. Then everything stopped.

On the opposite platform stood Lola. Her beaded costume shimmered in the spotlight. She smiled.

Lenny smiled.

They each caught a swinging trapeze and swung toward one another. They both did triples.

The crowd went wild! The applause grew until the tent could no longer hold it.

Again Lenny and Lola caught the trapezes.

Their eyes met and that's when the magic happened. Their hands left the bars and effortlessly they began to fly.

The crowd was spellbound.

"They're falling!" screamed a woman in the second row. But they did not fall. They continued to fly around the tent in gentle arcs, then glided down to the open door and out into the purple night.

Moonlight shimmered on their costumes as they sailed among the stars.

People will talk about that night
for a long, long time.